BY:_____

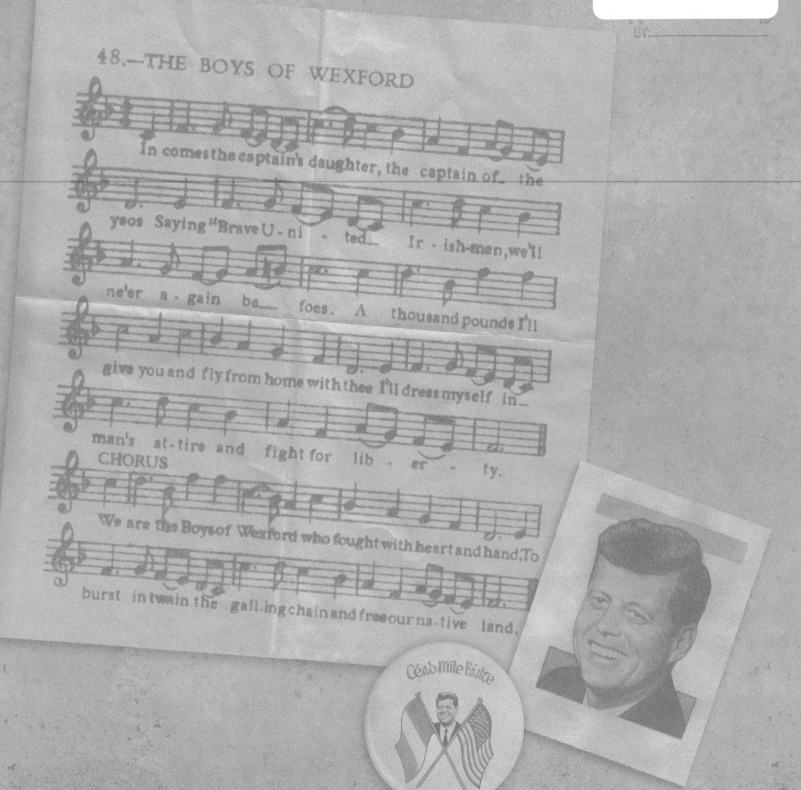

The radio crackled on the kitchen table:

"In 1848, on the quay of New Ross in County Wexford, President John F. Kennedy's great-grandfather Patrick Kennedy boarded a famine ship for the long journey to America. And now, 115 years later, the White House has confirmed that President Kennedy will return to his ancestral home, New Ross, as part of his extended trip to Ireland."

He wasn't president when he was here. . . .
That's the way he wanted to be, I think. He wanted to be just one of ourselves.

— Josie Grennan, a Kennedy cousin

For Ella and Julia — they haven't invented that word yet and you know why. Xx

And for Christopher, Sean-Felipe, Santiago, and Katie, the next generation of Tubridys — keep it goofy.

Enormous gratitude to Deirdre and Maria at Walker Books, who warmly and kindly and with great humor cajoled me hither and thither to breathe life into Patrick and his world.

Also, thank you to P.J. for giving me the privilege of having his beautiful art associated with my simple story.

❖ R. T.

For Ronan, Teresa, Rory, Oscar, and Flora

With thanks to my models, particularly Paddy, Dermot, and Saibh

Thanks also to Sam, Ben, Evie, Barbara, Julia, and Ryan

I also want to acknowledge the generous help I received from Patrick Grennan of the Kennedy Homestead Visitor Centre, Dunganstown, County Wexford, and Sam Rubin of the John F. Kennedy Presidential Library and Museum in Boston.

❖ P.J. L.

Song lyrics to "The Boys of Wexford" reproduced with kind permission from the President's Office Files, John F. Kennedy Presidential Library and Museum.

Painting of The Irish Times *newspaper included with thanks to The Irish Times.*

All reasonable efforts have been made to trace the copyright holders and secure permissions for the use of material used herein.
The publisher will be happy to incorporate any missing acknowledgments in any future edition of this book.

PATRICK
AND THE
PRESIDENT

RYAN TUBRIDY
P.J. LYNCH

CANDLEWICK PRESS

Patrick had been trying to teach his dog, Bing, to sit when the news was broadcast: the thirty-fifth president of the United States of America would be coming to Wexford, Ireland — Patrick's very own hometown.

Patrick's daddy began leaping around the room with delight. His mam was near-giddy with excitement, and even Bing was definitely in no mood to stay still — now he was up on his hind legs, dancing round the kitchen.

"Well, that's settled so!" Patrick's daddy said. "'Himself' is coming. There'll be some commotion that week. Can you imagine what this will do to the town?"

"Oh, I just knew he'd come," said Patrick's mam with a sigh, looking dreamily off into the distance. "Sure, his people are from here, so why wouldn't he? I'm only dying to see him. He's like something from the movies!"

At school that Monday, there was only one topic at recess:
the president's upcoming visit.

"His helicopter is the size of a spaceship," proclaimed Victor Delaney,
who had every intention of visiting the moon by his twelfth birthday.

Carmel Minihan told anyone who would listen that she knew
for a fact that the president's car was as long as two houses.
"The windows are *this* thick," she said, her arms stretched out
as far as they could go.

Even shy John Synott got in his tuppence worth: Secret Service
agents wore X-ray glasses. "True story!" he said with a flourish.

It was normally chilly in Patrick's school, even in April, but that morning at assembly the air was hot and humming with anticipation. The children knew something was up.

Standing at the front of the room, Father Power signaled for calm and quiet, getting both much faster than usual. With a small cough to clear his throat, he addressed his young audience. "As you well know, boys and girls, President Kennedy is coming to Ireland. More precisely, he is coming home — his family was from here in New Ross. When the president lands at O'Kennedy Park, he will be greeted by a choir of schoolchildren." He paused. "And *you,* boys and girls . . ." Father Power paused again and beamed. "*You* will be the choir!"

The room erupted into an enormous chorus of cheers,
the children's eyes and smiles wide and bright.

When the first flurry of excitement died down,
Patrick raised his hand.
"Excuse me Father, is this . . . true?
Will we really be there? All of us? Singing?
For the president of the United States?"
Five questions in one breath, a new record for Patrick.

But Father Power didn't mind.
"Yes, Patrick," he said, "each and every one of you."

A new burst of frenzied chitter-chatter filled the room.
The president! What will we sing, do you think?
Will we have to wear uniforms?
What will he be like?

Patrick couldn't wait to get home.

He raced through the door to his mam — almost tripping over Bing, hot on his heels — and fourteen different things tumbled out of his mouth all at once.

"A-a-a-and . . . I might actually get to *meet* the president!" Patrick finally concluded, breathless and flushed.
His mam gently pressed a cool hand to his cheek and then, bursting at the seams with pride, scooped Patrick up into her arms.

By the time Patrick's daddy came home from his job at the Ritz Cinema, the whole house was abuzz with Kennedy chat. Thanks to the newsreels they showed before each film, Patrick's daddy knew everything there was to know about it.

"You'll never guess who I bumped into today!" said Patrick's daddy. "Only President Kennedy's nearest relatives in Ireland—the Ryan girls! So it seems the Ryans are hosting a big tea party at the homestead in Dunganstown, and they'll be serving cake and sandwiches to the president and his sisters." Patrick's daddy paused dramatically.

His wife gave him a friendly shove. "Oh now, come on, out with it! This isn't a movie you're in now!"

"Well," he replied with a grin, "I offered up young Patrick's services to help at the tea party."

Patrick opened his mouth. Closed it. Opened it.

"You look like a little goldfish!" his daddy said with a laugh. "I take it you're available, then?"

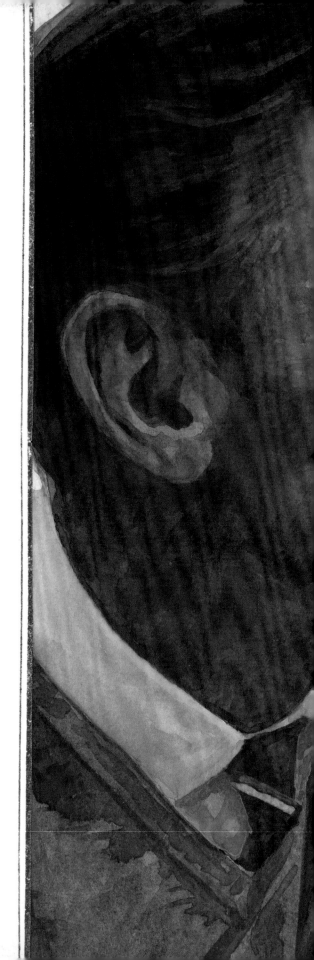

For the next three weeks, Patrick stayed late after school with all the other boys and girls, practicing and perfecting the three songs they would perform. Lying in bed at night, staring up at his ceiling, Patrick would mumble the words: *"We are the Boys of Wexford, who fought with heart and hand. . . ."*

And in the morning, when he woke, the lyrics were already on his lips: *"In comes the captain's daughter, the captain of the Yeos, saying, 'Brave United Irishmen, we'll ne'er again be foes.'"*

At the weekend, Patrick went to the Ryans' to rehearse his Swiss roll responsibilities:

- Take one strawberry Swiss roll.
- Slice it into six equal parts.
- Place it neatly onto a fine china plate.

"Easy now. A bit more gently than that, good lad!"

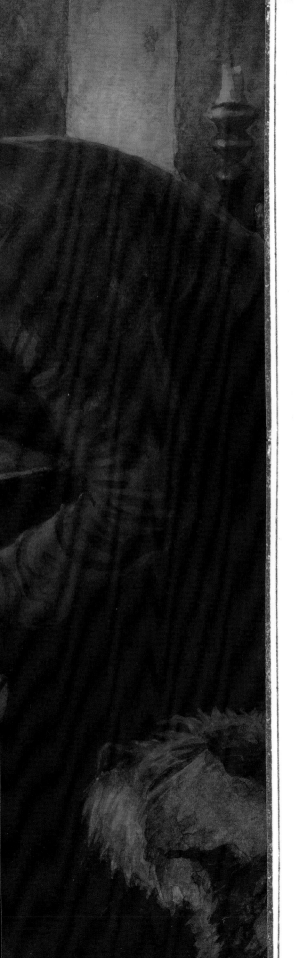

At last, at 8:03 p.m. on June 26, the president landed in Ireland.

Patrick and his parents huddled around the radio and listened to President de Valera welcome Ireland's most famous returning emigrant son, describing him as "a distinguished scion of our race, who has won first place amongst his fellow countrymen, first in a nation of one hundred and eighty million."

Patrick looked at his father. "Did he say one hundred and eighty million? Are there really one hundred and eighty *million* people in America?"

"Yes, son," replied his daddy. "Now, listen closely. It doesn't get much better than this for one of our own."

A day later, on the morning of the president's visit to New Ross, Patrick woke at 6:00 a.m. It felt like Christmas; he'd barely managed twenty minutes' sleep.

Patrick was never so careful getting dressed.

He kept a very giddy Bing at arm's length while his mother made the final checks: she smoothed his cowlick, polished the dried mud off his left shoe, then licked a tissue and dabbed at his face.

And, with one final *"RightbyeseeyoulateryeahIknowIknow!,"* Patrick was hurtling out the door, heading for O'Kennedy Park.

At O'Kennedy Park, everyone's gaze was fixed firmly on the sky.

Waiting.

Suddenly, the silence was shattered. Carmel let out a yelp and gestured wildly to the sky. "There it is! He's coming!"

Sure enough, a roar and a *hummmmm-brummm* filled the sky, and soon after, an enormous green metal bird slowly descended toward the field. Within seconds of the motor stopping, businesslike men with cameras around their necks and notebooks in their hands emerged.

"They're the journalists," whispered Victor knowingly.

When a second helicopter landed, another lot of men emptied out, but this time in tan coats and jet-black sunglasses.

"You see, didn't I tell ye?" said John, thrilled, unable to take his eyes off the men.

But, still . . . no sign of the president.

Five long minutes later, the air felt like it was vibrating and a rumble ripped through the clouds. The craft landed, and as the whirring blades slowed, the door opened and the steps came down. Patrick stood on his tippy-toes and squinted to focus until finally he saw . . .

Himself.

The president of the United States.

The children had just burst into "The Boys of Wexford"
when Carmel started nudging Patrick in the back.
The president was approaching.

The children suddenly sang louder — reaching deeper and deeper
for every note. As they neared the end of the song, Patrick could
just about see the president, standing at Father Power's shoulder;
he wanted to join in for a verse! Soon, the children's voices
were intermingled with the deep baritone of President Kennedy,
who grinned his way through the tune, patting freshly shampooed
heads and shaking little outstretched hands.

Patrick reached up — they all did — wanting so desperately to know
what it would feel like to shake the president's hand. . . .

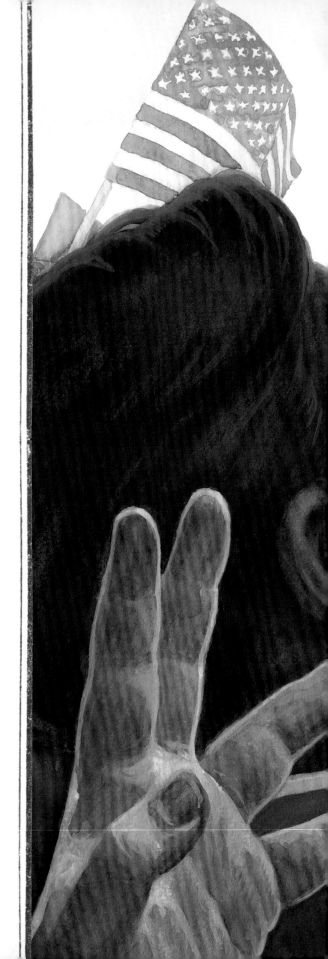

But a tap on the shoulder pulled the president away,
reminding him that he had a lot to fit in that day.
So, with a big wave and a last flash of that movie-star grin,
the president made his way to the waiting fleet of
enormous black cars.

"That's some car," said John, transfixed.

"I think it might well be the size of two houses!" said Victor,
whose eyes did not leave the entourage until the very
last wheel drove out of sight.

And then Carmel cried because she never got to meet
President Kennedy, and because it was all over.
The singing.
The excitement.

For Patrick, however, there was still *one* more chance.

Patrick raced home to change into a crisp shirt and tie (new)
and freshly ironed shorts (old), and from there he made his way
to Dunganstown, to his Swiss roll.

At the homestead, the world's press was waiting.
Mrs. Ryan was on the ball: there were starched doilies,
freshly cut triangle sandwiches, a smoked salmon centerpiece,
and a cake, emblazoned with a picture of the president himself.

Inside the house, Patrick found a corner of the kitchen where
he could concentrate. He plucked a knife from the drawer and,
holding his breath, began delicately to cut the Swiss roll.

One . . . two . . . three . . . four . . .
nearly there . . .
five!

Phew!

Perfect.

Outside, Patrick could see the Sunday-best-clad legs
and elbows of those clamoring to meet Himself.
He tried to make his way through the crowds, but there
was no clear path. Suddenly, his chest began to feel tight . . .
he only had this one chance.

"Over here, Patrick!" a voice called out. Patrick turned,
and there was his daddy, arms outstretched, grinning.
"This way, son!"

Carefully protecting his plate of cake, with his daddy
steering his elbow, Patrick dipped and dodged his way
to the front of the pack, finally emerging out into the yard.

Patrick breathed a huge sigh of relief before looking up . . .

and his eyes met those of President Kennedy. Time slowed down.
As if in a dream, Patrick held out his hand . . .

and JFK took it. And shook it.

"Is that for me?" the president asked, smiling and nodding toward
the Swiss roll. Patrick looked at his plate, looked back up at Himself,
and offered up his perfectly sliced Swiss roll. The tanned hand reached
out and picked up a slice.

"Well, that is just delicious. Thank you, young man."

The president was then quickly swallowed up by
the crowd.

Patrick's legs felt like jelly, his head dizzy.

His parents found him soon enough (and Bing did, too,
of course).

"Don't ever wash that lucky hand of yours!"
said Patrick's mam, hugging him to her,
while his daddy roared laughing.

They told the story of Patrick and the president
many times that day . . .
        and the next . . .
            and for a long, long time to come.

JOHN F. KENNEDY'S
1963 VISIT TO IRELAND

In 1960, forty-three-year-old John Fitzgerald Kennedy was elected president of the United States—the youngest person and the first ever Catholic to hold that office. On November 22, 1963, JFK was assassinated in Dallas, Texas. The death of this charismatic and energetic world leader was mourned the world over, and to this day he is considered one of the best-loved figures in American history.

John F. Kennedy always had close personal ties to Ireland. In the late 1840s, during the devastating potato famine, all eight of his great-grandparents left Ireland and immigrated to Boston, Massachusetts, where several family members became successful politicians. JFK treasured his Irish heritage, and after his presidential inauguration, he was determined to return to his ancestral home and walk in the footsteps of his forebears.

In April 1963, it was announced in Ireland that the American president was coming to visit. His trip was planned with military precision, and at every stop along his four-day trip, tens of thousands of people flocked to catch a glimpse of him. For a whole generation of Irish people, JFK's visit to Ireland became a momentous and unforgettable occasion in their lives.

"This is not the land of my birth, but it is the land for which I hold the greatest affection." —John F. Kennedy

The motorcade of President John F. Kennedy makes its way down crowd-lined O'Connell Street during his visit to Dublin.

JUNE 26, 1963 — DAY ONE

Dublin

At 8:00 p.m., Air Force One touches down at Dublin Airport. JFK is greeted by President Éamon de Valera and Taoiseach (Prime Minister) Seán Lemass. The Irish and American presidents both make short, formal speeches. With a twenty-five-man motorcycle escort, they then make their way to Áras an Uachtaráin in Phoenix Park, the residence of the Irish president. As the motorcade passes through the city center, more than 60,000 people line O'Connell Street to catch a glimpse of Kennedy.

JUNE 27, 1963 — DAY TWO

New Ross

JFK travels by helicopter to O'Kennedy Park in New Ross, County Wexford. From the air, he sees the word FÁILTE (WELCOME) spelled out by the shapes of children from the local school. A smiling and waving Kennedy is greeted by the Artane Boys' Band, and a choir of three hundred schoolchildren sings "The Boys of Wexford," known to be a favorite of the president's. The president walks over and joins in on the second chorus, causing one American photographer to tear up. Afterward, Kennedy shakes hands with as many schoolchildren as he can reach. Later, addressing the crowds at the quays in New Ross, JFK says, "I am glad to be here. It took 115 years to make this trip. And six thousand miles. And three generations. And I am proud to be here."

John F. Kennedy interacts with a child in the crowd while he visits his family's ancestral home in Dunganstown.

Dunganstown

JFK is driven to the Kennedy family homestead in Dunganstown, County Wexford. He is greeted by his distant cousin Mary Ryan and meets many more members of the extended Ryan and Kennedy families. After visiting with his cousins, JFK admires the feast that has been prepared for him outside: scones, Swiss rolls, sandwiches, and tea. There is even a large cake with his image on the icing. Kennedy remarks, "We want to drink a cup of tea to all the Kennedys who went and all the Kennedys who stayed."

Wexford Harbour

At the Wexford harborside, Kennedy lays a wreath in memory of Wexford-born commodore John Barry, America's first commissioned naval officer.

Dublin: Iveagh House

Kennedy attends a state dinner and reception at the Department of External Affairs, Iveagh House, Saint Stephen's Green, in his honor.

JUNE 28, 1963 — DAY THREE

Cork

Kennedy travels to Cork by helicopter and attends a reception in his honor.

Dublin: Arbour Hill

Kennedy returns to Dublin and visits Arbour Hill Cemetery, where he places a wreath on the graves of the executed leaders of the 1916 Easter Rising, becoming the first foreign head of state to honor them in a formal ceremony.

Leinster House

Kennedy addresses a Joint Sitting of the Houses of the Oireachtas (Legislature) in Leinster House. A huge crowd gathers outside, awaiting a glimpse of the president.

Dublin Castle

Kennedy makes his way to Saint Patrick's Hall, in Dublin Castle, where he receives honorary degrees from both the National University of Ireland and Dublin University.

JUNE 29, 1963 — DAY FOUR

Galway

On his visit to Galway, Kennedy tells the gathered crowd, "If the day was clear enough, and if you went down to the bay and you looked west, and your sight was good enough, you would see Boston, Massachusetts."

Limerick

Kennedy greets crowds at Greenpark Racecourse, in Limerick.

Shannon

Before his departure from Shannon Airport, Kennedy remarks, "I wish I could stay here for another week, or another month."

John F. Kennedy is served tea and cake by his distant cousin Mary Ryan at his Dunganstown homestead.